First published 1995 by Walker Books Ltd
87 Vauxhall Walk, London SE11 5HJ

© 1995 Michelle Cartlidge

Printed in Hong Kong

ISBN 0-7445-3939-0

Teddy's Cat

Michelle Cartlidge

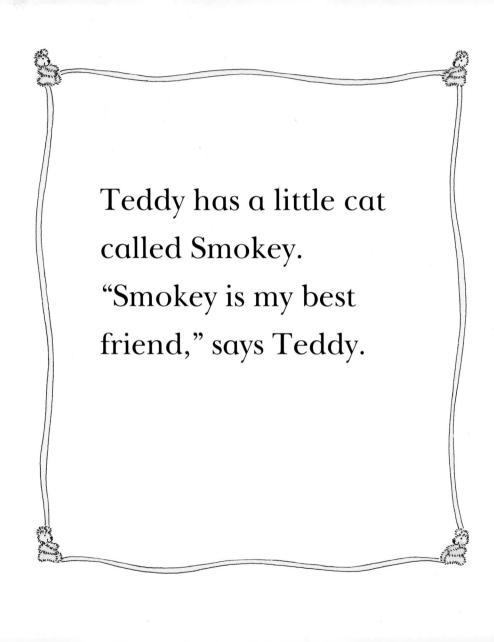

Teddy has a little cat
called Smokey.
"Smokey is my best
friend," says Teddy.

Teddy loves his cat
and takes good care
of her.

"Come on, Smokey.
It's time for your
breakfast," he calls.

Smokey has a toy mouse
and a little ball.
But she likes to play with
Mummy Bear's wool.
"Oh dear," says Teddy.
"What a tangle!"

Teddy takes Smokey
out into the garden
to play. Smokey likes
to chase the butterflies
but she can't catch
them.

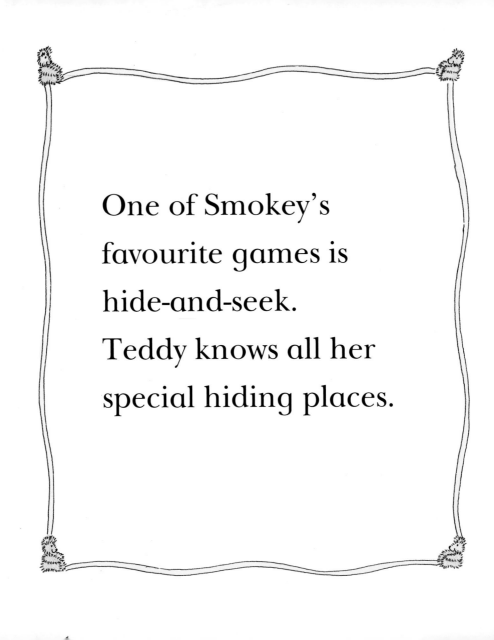

One of Smokey's
favourite games is
hide-and-seek.
Teddy knows all her
special hiding places.

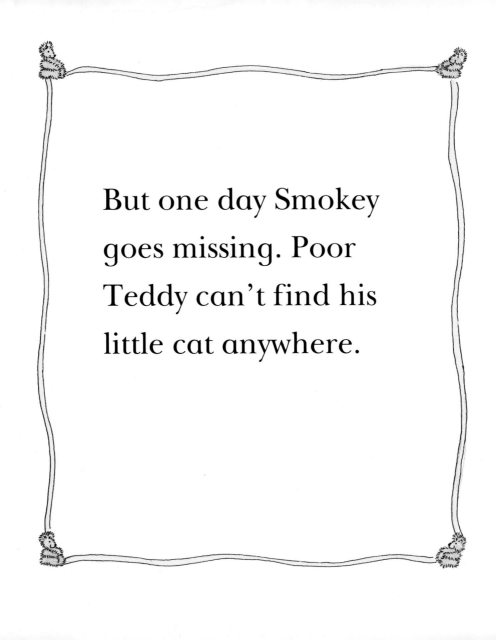

But one day Smokey goes missing. Poor Teddy can't find his little cat anywhere.

Mummy Bear opens
the airing cupboard.
"Look, Teddy. Smokey
wants to show you
something."

"Kittens!" says Teddy.
"They're beautiful!
What a clever cat you
are!"